GROSS GODS

HERCULES and the
Pooper-Scooper PERIL

WRITTEN BY
ILLUSTRATED B

Raintree is an imprint of Capstone Global Library Limited, a company
incorporated in England and Wales having its registered office at 264 Banbury
Road, Oxford, OX2 7DY — Registered company number: 6695582

www.raintree.co.uk
myorders@raintree.co.uk

Designed by Tracy McCabe
Production by Tori Abraham
Original illustrations © Capstone Global Library Limited 2020
Originated by Capstone Global Library Ltd

978 1 4747 8646 1

British Library Cataloguing in Publication Data
A full catalogue record for this book is available from the
British Library.

Acknowledgements
Design Elements: Shutterstock: Andrii_M, Anna Violet,
Nikolai Zaburdaev

Printed and bound in India

CONTENTS

CHAPTER ONE

TWELVE DARES

Hercules struts down the streets of Athens with his friends. He flips back his brown hair. He puffs out his muscular chest. He flexes his huge biceps as he swings his arms.

Hercules and his friends are all heroes. But he, Hercules, is the mightiest of them all! (Or so our hero thinks.)

"I once fought a giant," his friend Jason brags.

"Oh yeah?" Odysseus shouts. "The other day, I battled a cyclops!"

"That's nothing," Hercules boasts as he strikes a pose to show off his biceps. "I could pummel a giant with one hand while wrestling a cyclops with the other."

His friends shake their heads. Hercules always has to outdo them.

Then his friend Perseus brags, "I was dared to fight a monster with snakes for hair."

"Oh yeah?" Theseus shouts. "I was dared to fight a monster with a bull's head."

"That's nothing," Hercules boasts. He stops in the middle of the street and sticks out his chest as far as it can go. "I have never said no to a dare."

His friends all stop and turn and stare at each other.

"I will do a dare right now," Odysseus says. "Just name it!"

"I will do two," Jason brags, wanting to beat Odysseus.

"I will do three," Theseus states, wanting to outdo Jason.

"I will do four," Perseus proclaims, wanting to show up Theseus.

"I will do more than all of you combined." Hercules laughs as he flips back his hair. "I will do *eleven*!"

His friends look at each other, confused.

"But that's not how it works," Odysseus says.

"You're supposed to say that you will do five," Jason says.

"Then someone else will do six," Theseus adds.

"And when someone says they will do ten," Perseus explains, "then you can say you will do eleven."

Hercules puffs out his chest again. And again, he flexes his biceps as he flips back his hair ... again.

"Fine, then I will do twelve!" Hercules shouts. "What's my first challenge?"

With all their bragging and boasting, shouting and yelling, a large crowd has formed around the heroes. A young girl steps out of the gathering.

"Could you scoop out my cat's litter tray?" she asks.

"What?!" Hercules scoffs. "That's no challenge for a hero like me."

Hercules stands in the middle of the street. He sticks out his chest and pumps his biceps. Again and again and again. And yep, again.

As the crowd watches, people mumble.

"Why won't he take up the challenge?" someone asks.

"He must be afraid," someone says.

"He's a chicken," another teases. "Cluck! Cluck! Cl-uck!"

Soon, everyone in the crowd is flapping their arms and clucking like chickens. Even our hero's friends join in. "Cluck! Cluck! Cl-uck!"

Hercules flips his hair back one last time and growls, "Enough!"

Then he turns to the girl.

"Show me to your cat's litter," he says. "For I, Hercules, am the mightiest pooper scooper ever!"

The girl leads Hercules to a small hut just outside of town. His friends follow, and behind them the crowd of people gather.

"Just one second," the girl says as she enters the hut.

A moment later, she comes back out. She hands Hercules a large pooper-scooper.

"You'll need this." And then she adds, "Sir Pounce-A-Lot's litter tray is in the garden."

Hercules walks around the hut. In the garden, he sees what looks like a large sand pit. But our hero knows it is where Sir Pounce-A-Lot does his business. In the middle of it is a pile of steaming dung.

"That smells like cat poo," Jason says.

"Tastes like it, too," Odysseus adds.

"And it's still warm," Theseus says, holding his hand over.

"Sir Pounce-A-Lot must be nearby," Perseus says.

Just then, they hear a loud **RRROOOAAARRR!** Hercules turns, not to see a fluffy little kitten, but to see a fully-grown lion.

"Nice kitty," Hercules whispers as his friends back away.

Sir Pounce-A-Lot pulls back his paw. **WHACK!** He sends Hercules bouncing and rolling. Then he pounces on our hero. **THWUMP!**

"Get off, you crazy cat!" Hercules shouts.

Sir Pounce-A-Lot takes a quick swipe at Hercules.

"YEE-OOOWWW!" Our hero yells as his top is shredded.

"I'm just here to clean your litter tray," Hercules says, holding out the pooper-scooper.

The furry feline takes another swipe at Hercules.

Again, our hero yells **"YEE-OOOWWW!"** as his robe is shredded.

While Hercules staggers to his feet, Sir Pounce-A-lot pulls back his paw. **SMACK!** He sends Hercules rolling and tumbling. Our hero lands in the litter tray.

Then Sir Pounce-A-Lot pounces. **THWUMP!** The giant cat begins to scratch and kick up sand. He buries Hercules in his litter tray as if her were a giant turd.

Afterwards, Sir Pounce-A-Lot struts over to the girl. He purrs and nuzzles her.

Meanwhile, Hercules unburies himself. His clothes are shredded, and his hair is a mess. But he begins to scoop out stinky yellow clumps of sand and ever stinkier brown clumps.

CHAPTER TWO

THE SLIMY SLUG OF LERNEA

After changing his clothing, Hercules asks the crowd for his next challenge. A voice shouts, "Battle the Slimy Slug of Lernea."

"A slug?" Hercules scoffs. "How is that a challenge worthy of a hero like me?"

"It's super-duper slimy," someone else shouts.

"And it spits gobs of goo," another adds.

"Does it have claws?" Hercules asks.

People in the crowd shake their heads and mumble, "No".

"Then I will take up this challenge," Hercules shouts. "For I, Hercules, am the mightiest slug battler ever!"

The next day, Hercules and his friends leave Athens. They head towards the swamps of Lernea.

"Where is this Slimy Slug?" Hercules asks as they stomp through the bog.

Suddenly **SPLAT!** Hercules lifts up his foot. It is covered in brown, dripping ooze.

"That looks like slug poo," Theseus says.

"Smells like it too," Perseus adds, scrunching up his nose.

"Tastes like it too," Odysseus says.

"Over there," Jason says, pointing towards a pool of muck. "I can see it."

"Quick, behind that bush," Hercules tells his friends.

From their hiding spot, they can see a giant slug, about the size of a barn. It is bathing in a pool of muck.

"It has nine eyes," Hercules says. "It will see me sneaking up on it."

"Heroes don't sneak!" Perseus says.

"They just club things," Theseus says.

Hercules pulls out his pooper-scooper and shouts. "I am the mighty Herc–"

As he shouts, all of the slug's nine eyes turn to our hero. Then the beast belches. **BAAAWWKKK!** It spits a glob of goo at Hercules which smacks him in the face.

Hercules bounces backwards until he lands in a puddle of mud. **SPLOOSH!**

"Got any other ideas?" Hercules asks his friends.

"Hmm … maybe don't let it hit you in the face with goo again?" Odysseus says.

"Yeah, that's a good idea." Jason nods.

"Great!" Hercules grumbles. "Thanks for the help."

Hercules charges the slug. Again, all nine of its eyes turn towards our mighty hero.

When Hercules gets close, the slug lifts its tail out of the mud. **WHACK!** Hercules is sent bouncing and skipping across the marsh.

SPLOOSH! Again, he lands in a puddle of mud.

"I don't know how to defeat this monster," Hercules shouts to his friends.

"The dare was to battle the Slimy Slug of Lernea," Perseus says.

"Not to defeat the Slimy Slug of Lernea," Odysseus adds.

"Then dare two is complete!" Hercules shouts. "Let's get out of this swamp."

Just then, another gob of goo **SMACKS** Hercules.

"Why don't you walk behind us," Theseus says.

"Yeah, you smell like slug sick," Perseus adds.

On their way home, someone dares Hercules to bathe with a giant pig.

As our hero lounges in brown, smelly muck, his friends watch.

"Does he know it's not just mud in that pig sty?" Odysseus says.

"Yeah, it's a bit like bathing at the public baths," Perseus adds.

"Everybody wees in them," Theseus says.

"From the smell," Jason says, "I think that pig has more than weed in his bath."

OINK! OINK!

Next, Hercules is dared to capture the giant porcupine of Cerynitis. He completes the challenge, but only after being pierced in the bum by a giant porcupine quill.

"Just bend over," Odysseus tells Hercules.

"We will pull it out on the count of three," Perseus says.

"One," Theseus says. "Two."

"Pull!" Jason shouts.

"YEE-OOOWWW!!!" Hercules screams.

For his fifth dare, Hercules is challenged to scrub clean the statue of Athena. She is the goddess of wisdom, and her statue stands in Athens' city square. All day pigeons fly overhead and leave their droppings on the statue. And all day, our hero scrubs and scrubs.

"It's a bit like rain," Perseus says.

"Thick, chunky rain," Theseus says.

"That tastes like poo," Odysseus says, while sticking his tongue out.

"You missed a spot," Jason says, pointing at the statue.

Hercules grumbles as he **SCRUB! SCRUB! SCRUBS!**

CHAPTER THREE

POOPER SCOOPER

Upon returning to Athens, Hercules shouts to the crowd, "What is my sixth dare?"

"Clean my stable," a farmer replies.

Our hero's shoulders slump. "More poo? I'm filthy from head to toe. I'm not sure I can take much more!"

"But aren't you, Hercules, the mightiest pooper scooper ever?" the farmer asks.

"Why yes, I am!" our hero proclaims. "So show me this stable of yours."

The farmer leads Hercules and his friends to the stable.

"Wow, look at that!" Theseus says.

"How long has it been since this stable's been cleaned?" Perseus asks.

"About thirty years or so," the farmer replies.

Odysseus takes a long, deep breath in through his nose. **SNIFFFFFFFFFFFFFFFFF!** "Yep, I'd say he's about right, give or take a year."

"That pile of poo must be fifty metres high," Odysseus says.

Everyone is looking up, up towards the sky. Next to the stable stands a leaning tower of horse manure.

"How are you going to clean that mess up?" Jason asks Hercules.

"I will shovel it into those wagons," he says, pointing to a group of empty wagons. "You four can haul the poo away."

As Hercules digs in, his friends line up a row of wagons in front of the tower.

"Wouldn't it be better to start from the top?" the farmer asks.

Hercules doesn't pay any attention to him. He scoops out huge shovelfuls of number two from the bottom of the tower. He throws them behind him into the wagons. He shovels and scoops, and as he works, poo and dung, manure and faeces, fly everywhere. His friends hide behind the wagons to avoid the spray.

Hercules is about halfway through the base of the manure tower when it starts to teeter. Then it totters a bit.

"It's gonna topple," Perseus yells as the tower of poo sways back and forth.

"Run for it!" Odysseus shouts.

Then suddenly, the tower teeters one last time. It falls towards the fleeing heroes. The manure **SPLATS** down onto the line of waiting wagons, filling them up to the top.

"That was close," Odysseus says.

"We almost got buried in manure," Jason says.

"But where's Hercules?" Theseus asks.

"There!" Perseus says.

From the base of the tower, a hand rises out of the poo. Then a second hand, holding a pooper-scooper, pops out. Next comes a head, poking out of the dung.

It is Hercules, covered from head to toe in horse manure. Our hero joins his friends.

"Another dare complete!" he shouts.

"I wish someone would dare you to bathe," Theseus says.

"You smell worse than Hephaestus' toilet," Perseus adds.

Hercules and his friends strut back into town. As our hero puffs out his chest, he asks the crowd, "What is my next challenge?"

A man dares Hercules to sharpen the horns of a giant bull from Crete.

"Are they pointy enough now?" Hercules asks while fleeing from the monstrous bull.

Just then, the bull's horns rip through Hercules' robe. Our hero is poked in the bum.

"YE-OOOWWW!!!" he shouts.

"Yep, that'll do," the man says.

Then Hercules is dared to let himself be swallowed by a giant snake.

"This was a bad idea," Perseus says.

"How's he going to get out of its belly?" Jason asks.

"There's only one way out," Odysseus adds.

"And that's not going to be pretty," Theseus says.

CHAPTER FOUR

ARES' UNDERWEAR

Back in Athens, Hercules stands in front of the crowd. Flies buzz around our smelly hero. People gag and wrinkle their noses in disgust. But he does not let that bother him.

"I have battled the Slimy Slug and been pooed out of a giant snake," Hercules says. "No challenge is too great for me!"

"Then steal Ares' underwear!" someone from the crowd shouts.

"Seriously?" Hercules asks. "The god of war never changes his tighty-whities."

"Seriously!" the crowd yells back.

"Okay, then," our hero shouts. "For I, Hercules, am the mightiest underwear stealer ever."

The next day, Hercules and his friends head to Mount Olympus. It is the tallest peak in all of Greece and also the home of the gods.

The heroes climb up and up until they are above the clouds. In front of them stands the home of the gods.

Hercules and his friends enter the gods' house. First they walk through the living room, next the kitchen, and then the dining area. They enter a long corridor. On each side are six doors, and above each door is the name of one of the gods.

They hurry past Apollo's door. A blinding light shines from the room.

Next they run past Hephaestus' door. And just in time too. A loud **PTTTHHHBBBBB!** erupts from inside followed by a blast of fire. It shoots all the way across the hallway and into Artemis' room. She is goddess of the hunt.

"If you fart in my room one more time," she shouts, "I will plug your bottom with an arrow!"

When they reach Ares' room, they find it empty.

Perseus scratches his head. "Where do you think he is?"

"Probably in the gym," Hercules replies, flexing one of his arms. "He's always been jealous of my biceps."

Our hero's friends just shake their heads.

At the end of the corridor, they take a left. That leads to the gym, where they spot Ares. He stands in front of a mirror, puffing out his chest and flexing his arms.

"What shall I do?" Hercules asks his friends.

"I have an idea," Odysseus says. "Go and distract him."

Hercules steps into the gym and shouts to Ares, "You call those biceps?"

The god of war turns to our hero and flips back his hair. "You call that shaggy mop on your head hair?" Ares scowls.

Hercules puffs up his chest. "Your pecs look like udders," Hercules tells the god of war.

The pair stand, facing each other. They pump their biceps. They stick out their chests. They throw their hair back and forth.

After a while, both of them are starting to sweat and pant.

"This is hard work," Ares says. He grabs his water bottle and takes a big swig.

Suddenly the god of war's face turns bright red. His ears, too. Then his tummy gurgles. It grumbles and groans.

Ares doubles over in pain and crosses his legs. "I must go to the toilet," he moans.

The god of war darts out of the gym.

"What did you do?" Hercules asks Odysseus.

Odysseus holds up a bottle of Zeus' ToXXXic Hot Sauce. "I took this from the kitchen," he says, "and filled Ares water bottle with it."

"Now go and get his underwear!" Perseus shouts.

Hercules runs to the bathroom. When he opens the door, the stench nearly knocks him over. "Phew!!"

"UGHH! It smells like a poo has farted." Hercules coughs.

Then he hears Ares, grunting and groaning, spluttering and spitting.

The god of war is in the last cubicle. Peeking under the door, Hercules sees Ares' underwear around his ankles. Our hero runs over and reaches under the cubicle's curtain.

"Hey!" Ares shouts as Hercules pulls his underwear away. "That's my only pair!"

FWOOSH!

With Ares' underwear in hand, Hercules races out of the room. His friends join him as he escapes through the gym and down the corridor. Soon, they are outside and climbing down Mount Olympus.

When they have returned to Athens, Hercules holds up Ares' underwear proudly.

"Another dare completed," he shouts.

For his tenth dare, Hercules is challenged to compete in a cow-pat-eating contest.

"Does he know what those are made of?" Odysseus asks.

"Cow?" Perseus asks.

"Not exactly," Theseus says.

"He's just eaten his tenth one," Jason says. "I think he's going to win."

For his eleventh dare, Hercules is challenged to hold up Zeus' bottom for a day. Usually this task is Atlas' job. Atlas is a super strong Titan who once angered Zeus by saying the ruler of the gods had a giant bum. So he was punished to hold it up for eternity.

"You picked a good day to relieve me," Atlas says. "Last night was taco night on Mount Olympus, and Zeus likes his hot sauce."

Suddenly a loud, gaseous *TTTHHHBBB!* erupts from the buttocks.

"Ewww," Hercules gasps. "It smells like baked beans."

CHAPTER FIVE

WALKING THE DOG

"Finally, just one more dare," Hercules shouts. Then he turns to the crowd and asks, "What shall my last challenge be?"

"Take Hades' dog Cerberus for a walk," someone shouts out.

"That will be easy," Hercules says, puffing out his chest. "For I, Hercules, am the best dog walker ever."

Hades is god of the Underworld.

To reach the Underworld, people travel through the sewers under Athens. Hercules lifts up a manhole cover in the middle of the road.

Before he jumps down, he asks his friends, "Are you joining me?"

The friends shake their heads.

"That's where all the number one goes," Perseus says.

"And the number two after people flush their toilets," Theseus says.

"And it smells," Jason adds, wrinkling up his nose.

"Probably tastes gross, too," Odysseus adds.

"Fine, I will go by myself," Hercules says.

Our hero jumps down into the sewer and lands in a dark tunnel.

Running through the middle of the passageway is the River Stinx. It is said that anyone who touches its brown, lumpy water will stink forever.

Hercules follows the river, and it leads him to the Underworld. But our hero keeps as close to the walls of the tunnel as possible to avoid its foulness.

Hercules walks and walks. Every now and then, there is a loud **FLUSH!** A shower of yellow water with big brown chunks then falls on him.

"I should have brought an umbrella," Hercules grumbles, as – **FLUSH!** – he is drenched for the umpteenth time.

After hours of trudging through the sewers, Hercules reaches the tunnel's end. Before him is the entrance to a large cavern, the Underworld.

In front of the doorway sits a giant dog with not one, not two, but three heads. Behind the dog stands Hades. He holds a lead out to Hercules.

"I hear you are going to take Cerberus for a walk," Hades says.

"Yes, I am," Hercules states, grabbing the lead from Hades.

"Have fun," Hades says with a chuckle.

Just then, Cerberus lunges forward, and Hercules is pulled off his feet.

Cerberus spins around and enters the Underworld. The giant pooch drags our hero behind him.

All around are bubbling yellow pools of foul water. From the ceiling hang stalactites that drip smelly brown ooze.

Cerberus drags Hercules splashing and splooshing through the reeking yellow pools.

As he whirls around, our hero **SLAMS!** and **SMACKS!** into the slimy brown stalactites. Around and around, Cerberus runs. All Hercules can do is hold on as he **SPLASHES** through bubbling pools and **SLAMS!** against the oozing stalactites.

Cerberus runs and runs and runs. He spins back towards the cave's entrance and darts down the tunnel.

Luckily for Hercules, he sees a large brownish log floating in the River Stinx. He leaps onto it and uses the log to ski along the river as Cerberus runs down the passageway.

At the end of the tunnel, Cerberus leaps up through the manhole. Hercules is dragged behind him. Our hero flies out of the sewers and lands in the middle of the street with a **THUMP.**

Hercules loses his grip on Cerberus' lead. The three-headed dog then disappears back down into the sewer.

Our hero stands up in the middle of the road. He is wobbling a bit. His clothes are stained. His hair is a mess. And he shouts, "My last dare is complete!"

As the crowd cheers, Hercules' friends gather around him.

"We have one more challenge for you," Odysseus says, holding up a hose.

Theseus, Perseus and Jason all hold poles with soapy sponges at one held.

"We dare you to bathe!" Jason laughs.

THE REAL MYTH

In Greek myths, Hercules was the son of Zeus and the strongest man alive. He was famous for completing 12 nearly-impossible tasks called labours. For *Hercules and the Pooper-Scooper Peril*, each of Hercules' 12 dares is based on one of these labours.

Labour 1: Slay the Nemean Lion, a beast with hide so thick, weapons could not harm it.

Labour 2: Slay the Hydra, a nine-headed monster.

Labour 3: Catch the Ceryneian Hind, an incredibly fast deer.

Labour 4: Capture the Erymanthian Boar, a giant pig that destroyed everything in its path.

Labour 5: Clean the Augean Stables, which had not been cleaned for 30 years.

Labour 6: Scare away the Stymphalian Birds, which had metal beaks and feathers.

Labour 7: Capture the Cretan Bull, a monstrous animal.

Labour 8: Tame the Mares of Diomedes, which were man-eating horses.

Labour 9: Steal the Golden Belt of Hippolyte, the queen of a tribe of warrior women called Amazons.

Labour 10: Steal the Cattle of Geryon, a giant with three heads, six arms and six legs.

Labour 11: Steal the Apples of the Hesperides, nymphs who were the daughters of the Titan Atlas.

Labour 12: Capture Cerberus, a three-headed hound that protected the Underworld.

GLOSSARY

Apollo god of sunlight, music and poetry in Greek and Roman mythology

Ares god of war in Greek mythology

Artemis goddess of the moon, wild animals and hunting in Greek mythology

Athena Greek goddess of wisdom

bicep large muscle at the front of the upper arm

bog area of wet, spongy land

cyclops one-eyed giant

manure waste from animals in stables and barns

stable farm building where horses are kept

Underworld in myths, the place where spirits of the dead go

Zeus chief god, ruler of the sky and weather, and husband of Hera in Greek mythology

The myths of Ancient Greece are full of exciting challenges, deeds and heroes. We've asked some terrific authors to write some new adventures based on the ancient myths. They retell the exploits of your favourite heroes, like Hercules and Perseus and Jason, but in a totally different way. A gross and gruesome and disgusting way! Crack open a book from GROSS GODS, and you'll be inspired to be an epic hero. You might also be inspired to have a shower and clean out the fluff from between your toes!

Read on!

AUTHOR

Blake Hoena grew up in central Wisconsin, USA, where he wrote stories about robots conquering the moon and trolls lumbering around the woods behind his parents' house. He now lives in Minnesota, USA, and continues to make up stories about things like space aliens and superheroes. He has written more than 70 chapter books and graphic novels for children.

ILLUSTRATOR

Ivica Stevanovic is an illustrator, comic artist and graphic designer. He has published a huge number of illustrations in textbooks and picture books. Apart from working on illustrations for children's books, Ivica draws comics, and his speciality is graphic novels. His best-known graphic novel is *Kindly Corpses*. Ivica lives with his wife, Milica, and their two daughters, Katarina and Teodora, in Veternik, Serbia.

FOR MORE
DISGUSTING STORIES,
CHECK OUT...

GRIMM
AND
GROSS

nly from Raintree